K A M E H A M E H A

КАМЕН

AMEHA

The Warrior King of Hawai'i

SUSAN MORRISON

ILLUSTRATED BY KAREN KIEFER

A Latitude 20 Book

UNIVERSITY OF HAWAI'I PRESS

Honolulu

© 2003 Susan Morrison

Illustrations © 2003 Karen Kiefer

All rights reserved

Printed in the United States of America

08 07 06 05 04 03   6 5 4 3 2 1

Library of Congress Cataloging-in-Publication Data
A record of this book is on file.
ISBN 0-8248-2700-7

University of Hawai'i Press books are printed on
acid-free paper and meet the guidelines for permanence
and durability of the Council on Library Resources.

Design and composition by Jeff Clark and Megan Geer
at Wilsted & Taylor Publishing Services

Printed by Versa Press, Inc.

To my children and grandchildren

and the children of Hawaiʻi.

CONTENTS

PREFACE / ix

ACKNOWLEDGMENTS / xi

MAP OF HAWAI'I / xii

1

A Stormy Birth / 1

2

Flight to Safety / 5

3

Return to the King's Court / 9

4

The Naha Stone / 13

5

Warrior / 17

6

Floating Islands and Fire-Sticks / 21

7

War and Love / 27

8

King of Hawai'i / 31

9

A Friend from across the Sea / 37

10

Conquest / 41

11

The Campaign for Kaua'i / 45

12

King of All the Islands / 49

13

Kamehameha's Rule / 53

14

The Settled Years / 57

15

The Final Days / 61

AFTERWORD / 65

NOTES / 67

MELE INOA / 71

IMPORTANT DATES IN
KAMEHAMEHA'S LIFE / 73

GLOSSARY / 75

BIBLIOGRAPHY / 81

ABOUT THE AUTHOR
AND ILLUSTRATOR / 85

PREFACE

Looking back through history to an age before recorded time, we see a chief who was born on the island of Hawaiʻi. He grew up to become a great warrior, and, through battles and political wisdom, he united all the islands into a single kingdom in 1810.

The world first learned of Kamehameha through the journals of the voyagers on the ships of Captain James Cook, who arrived at the Hawaiian Islands in 1778. Later voyagers came on trading ships, and Hawaiʻi, under Kamehameha's rule, became an important Pacific trading port of interest to countries as far away as England, France, and Russia, as well as the United States.

The chants and stories of the ancient Hawaiians, passed down from generation to generation, and the firsthand accounts of early Western visitors present a picture of the life and times of Kamehameha. In 1820, Protestant missionaries arrived, less than a year after Kamehameha's death, and, together with Hawaiian historians, recorded events that were then in the recent past.

Mystery still surrounds many details concerning Kamehameha's birth and early years, and a certain amount of supposition has been necessary to complete the framework of the early part of his life.

ACKNOWLEDGMENTS

With heartfelt gratitude to Norma Gorst and the late Edward Joesting, who helped make this book possible. And a special thanks to my young manuscript reviewers, Kelly Morrison and Brita Hofwolt, whose comments and suggestions were of great value.

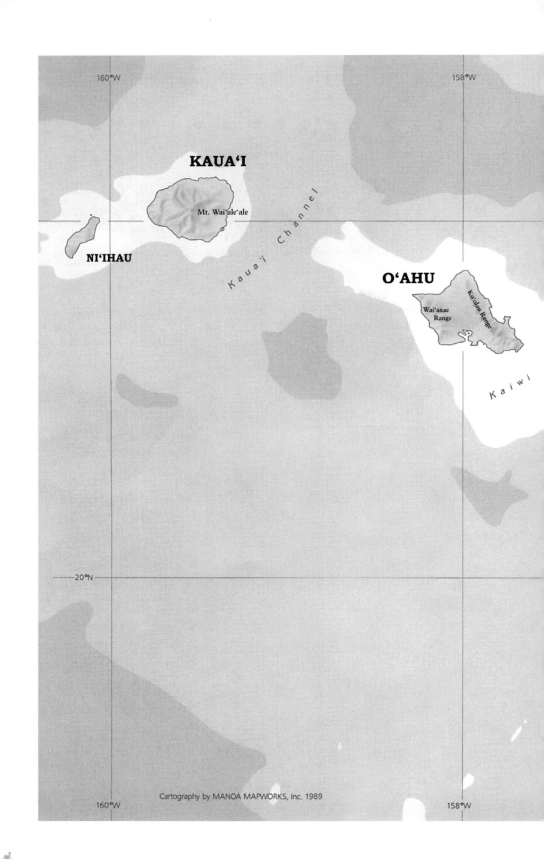

160°W · 158°W

KAUA'I

Mt. Wai'ale'ale

Kaua'i Channel

NI'IHAU

O'AHU

Wai'anae
Range

Ko'olau Range

Kaiwi

20°N

Cartography by MANOA MAPWORKS, Inc. 1989

160°W · 158°W

M A P   O F   H A W A I ' I

156°W

22°N

W — E

Channel

MOLOKA'I

West
Maui
Mtns.

MAUI

LĀNA'I

Haleakalā

Channel

KAHO'OLAWE

'Alenuihāhā

HAWAI'I

Kohala Mtns.

20°N

Mauna Kea

Mauna Loa

Kīlauea

156°W

C H A P T E R 1

A STORMY BIRTH

"We must hurry." Keku'iapoiwa's long black hair streamed past her face as the canoe surged through the swells toward Kohala. "I can feel the baby." She placed her hand beneath her heart. "He is ready to be born."

The canoe rounded the northern tip of the island of Hawai'i. Storm clouds rolled in front of the setting sun. Gusts of wind spun the sea into sharp peaks as the paddlers fought to keep a straight course. At last the canoe plunged through the surf and scraped the sand.

Darkness came with the rising wind. Thunder crashed and lightning pierced the sky. This was 'Ikuwā, the Hawaiian season of stormy weather. The comet, which had blazed in the sky the night before, lay behind the clouds. A chief would soon be born, for comets were signs of important births.

And Kekuʻiapoiwa's baby would be a chief. Not only were she and her husband, Keōua, *aliʻi,* chiefs of high birth, but many believed that the baby's true father was none other than Kahekili, the great warrior-chief of Maui. Half his body was tattooed black from head to foot, giving him a ferocious look. For sport, he liked to dive from a high cliff several hundred feet into the sea below. He was a fierce warrior in battle, and his name meant "thunder." A son of Kahekili would have great *mana,* divine power from the gods, and this baby would have double *mana,* since both Keōua and Kahekili were chiefs.

Now, on this night of ʻIkuwā, a baby's cry carried through the sound of surf and falling rain. The chiefess Kekuʻiapoiwa held the baby in her arms. She smiled as she watched him wave his tiny arms and legs. "You are like a little crab," she crooned. "I will call you Paiʻea. But now," she said sadly, "I must send you away so that Alapaʻi doesn't find you."

Alapaʻi, the king of Hawaiʻi, had been warned by a prophecy. His high priest, a *kahuna,* had predicted that a child would soon be born who would one day slay all rival chiefs and conquer all the islands. Alapaʻi ordered his warriors to find the baby and kill him. "Nip off the *wauke* bud while it is still young," he said to them, "lest it grow into a strong plant."

Kekuʻiapoiwa had made plans so that Alapaʻi wouldn't find her baby. She wrapped her little son in a cloth of *kapa* and laid him in a basket made of *olonā* fibers. She handed him to her trusted friend, Naeʻole, who was a chief of Kohala.

"Here, Naeʻole," she said. "We have no time to lose. Take the baby and run as fast as you can to the cliffs of ʻĀwini. Hurry, before we hear the pounding feet of Alapaʻi's men as they come to snatch the newborn chief. Take him there and hide him until it is safe for him to return to me. Hurry, and do not let yourself be seen. The rain will wash away your footprints."

FLIGHT TO SAFETY

Nae'ole ran through the soaked darkness, clutching the tiny bundle. He glanced warily about him as he ran. His breath came in gasps while his feet sought the trails that would lead him away from the sea to safety. He thought he could hear the thundering feet of his pursuers, but it was only the thudding of his heart. The baby slept secure in his arms, unaware of the dangers of the night. The storm lashed the runner's skin and lightning bursts lit the way before him. His feet slipped in the wet mud as he climbed.

The baby woke and let out a faint cry. "Shhh," he whispered, "we're almost there."

Exhausted, he wanted desperately to rest, but he had to keep going. The life of his young chief was in his hands. If he did not carry out his mission, both of them would die. The sky lightened as dawn approached. The storm, like a sleepy giant, began to quiet down. As the sun rose from behind the sea to the east, Naeʻole joyously took his last step up the steep trail and reached the top of the cliffs. He had reached ʻĀwini.

One day these words would be chanted in celebration of this brave journey:

> *Sheltered was the heavenly one at the land of ʻĀwini*
> *There the great chief Kamehameha was borne in the arms*
> *Like the feather of a goose*
> *To the sheer cliffs that stand there yet*
> *A dark shady spot to hide Paiʻea*
> *On the inaccessible cliff of ʻĀwini*

A woman waited at the opening of her shelter. She was a trusted cousin of the baby's mother.

"At last," she cried. "Have you brought me my little chief?"

"He is here," Naeʻole answered. He handed her the baby and collapsed on the ground. "We may be followed," he said, out of breath. "Where can we hide him?"

They placed the baby in a dark corner and covered his basket with *olonā* fibers so he could not be seen. During the day, they prayed away the rainbows, which were the signs of a chief's presence.

The king's men roamed the land searching for the newborn baby. They could not find him.

When the long day was near an end, the woman took the baby into her arms and murmured, "You are safe, my little one. I will care for you as though you were my own child."

The days and months passed safely, and, in the rain forests and valleys of the mountains, the boy spent his early years.

Nae'ole, who had brought him here, stayed with him and taught him the ways of life. He became the boy's *kahu*, or guardian. He carried the young chief on his shoulders as they explored the forests and the clear pools beneath the waterfalls.

"Someday," Nae'ole promised, "all this will be yours, and so you must know about the land."

He taught the boy to swim in the pools made by the waterfalls and to watch for the little fish that darted between the rocks. "Until you are grown," he cautioned, "you may not eat fish, for a bone may stick in your throat. But when you are big, you may eat all the fish you want."

Nae'ole showed him how to make kites of sticks covered with *kapa*, a cloth made from the bark of trees. He taught him to throw darts made from the feathers of birds. Pai'ea liked to slide down the mountains on the broad leaves of *kī* plants and to swing on the morning-glory vines. "If we use the land well, it will be good to us," Nae'ole told the boy. They watched the men in the valley tend their taro crops from which they made *poi*. Pai'ea liked *poi*, a thick, sticky paste he ate with his fingers. Other foods he ate were bananas, yams, coconuts, chicken, and pork.

Nae'ole and the boy spent many hours talking about the gods.

"Honor and obey the gods," Nae'ole told him, "and you can never do wrong."

He told Pai'ea about Kāne, the god of life, sunlight, and fresh water; Lono, the god of the harvest; and Kanaloa, the god of the sea. The most awesome god was Kū, the god of war, with his image of glaring eyes and savage teeth.

7

As they walked among the trees and the vines, Nae'ole said, "The woodsmen pray to the gods when they chop down the *koa* trees to hollow into canoes."

They listened to the little birds that sang their songs as they darted, bright as flowers, from tree to tree. From the small bodies of the yellow 'ō'ō, the scarlet 'i'iwi, and the golden *mamo* came the feathers for the capes of the chiefs.

The feathers of the *mamo* were reserved for kings.

The young boy gazed from the lonely mountain heights to the blue sea, which lay sparkling in the sun, many miles away.

"Someday," he promised Nae'ole, "I will have a cloak of *mamo* feathers."

RETURN TO THE

KING'S COURT

One day when Pai'ea was about five years old, Nae'ole said to him, "I have heard from your mother. She says the time has come to bring you back to her village. She says King Alapa'i is old now, and it is safe to bring you home."

"But Nae'ole," the boy answered, "this is my home, here with you in the mountains."

"Your home is with your people in the king's court. There you will learn the ways of the great chiefs and warriors. Do not be afraid. I will go with you," Nae'ole promised.

And so, Pai'ea left his mountains and valleys and traveled with Nae'ole to Kona by the sea.

His mother was overjoyed to have him back, and even Alapa'i welcomed him to his court. It was now that he was given the name he would bear the rest of his life, Kamehameha. His name meant "the lonely one," or "the one who has been set apart."

The years Kamehameha had spent far away in the mountains set him apart from the other children, but he soon became a leader among them. His mother smiled contentedly as she watched the other children follow him in their daily play.

He became a strong swimmer and could soon outrun his friends. As he grew older, he learned to paddle an outrigger canoe with long, powerful strokes. Surfing was his favorite sport. On his *koa* board, he learned to capture a high wave as it curled toward the shore.

Kamehameha liked to fish. Now that he was older, he was allowed to eat fish. He caught squid and eel in the reefs with his wooden fishing spear. Afterwards, on the beach, he liked to hurl his spear through the air. He pretended he was a great warrior battling his enemy.

After several years in the village in Kona, Kamehameha was sent to live with his uncle, Kalani'ōpu'u. Kalani'ōpu'u was a chief who could teach Kamehameha the ways of the *ali'i*, the royalty. He was fond of his nephew and told Kamehameha's mother, "I will look upon him as my son." So Kamehameha went to live in Ka'ū on the southeastern coast of Hawai'i, in the shadow of the great volcanic mountain, Mauna Loa.

Alapa'i, in the meantime, had become older and weaker, and when he died, Kalani'ōpu'u became the ruler of Hawai'i. Life at court became exciting, with many chiefs coming to pay respects to the new king. Kamehameha was now the nephew of the king of the island of Hawai'i.

"But remember," Kalani'ōpu'u told Kamehameha, "even though you are an *ali'i*, to be a chief, you must act like a chief."

In the evenings as they sat by the light of the torches, Kamehameha listened to the chants about warriors of the past. Dancers moved to the rhythm of the drums as they acted out the heroic deeds. He sat dreaming in the firelight and imagined a day when the chanters and dancers would celebrate the deeds of the great Kamehameha.

THE NAHA STONE

As Kamehameha grew older, he began to give up the games of his childhood.

"The time has come," Kalani'ōpu'u told him, "to begin your training. To be a chief, you must first prove yourself a warrior." He ordered Kekūhaupi'o, a brave and fearless warrior, to teach Kamehameha the arts of war.

Kamehameha was a good student. He was already muscular and agile from years of paddling, surfing, swimming, fishing, and mountain climbing. He knew how to wrestle and box, throw a spear, and hurl a heavy stone with a sling. Now he learned how to fight in battle.

A celebration marked the end of his training. During the

ceremony, a *kahuna* looked into the future and announced that Kamehameha would be a great warrior and that he would never die in battle.

At seventeen, Kamehameha felt strong and mighty. Over six feet tall, he had a proud, stern face with dark eyes that seemed to see beyond the horizon. With his powerful body and quick mind, he won many contests of strength and skill among his friends. He felt he possessed a great force within himself, not only from his own body, but from the gods as well.

He said, "I want to prove my strength against the Naha Stone."

The massive Naha Stone lay before a temple in Hilo. According to legend, the stone would be moved only by the tremendous strength of a chief who had extraordinary *mana*. He who overturned the stone would become the conqueror of the islands. The stone challenged all who approached it. Though many chiefs made the trip to Hilo, none had succeeded.

Kamehameha had known about this stone for many years and sometimes dreamed of it at night. He longed to try his strength.

"If ever this stone shall be moved," he said, "it will be by me."

He traveled over the mountains to Hilo with other warriors and chiefs from the king's court.

When Kamehameha came to the temple and saw the Naha Stone, he frowned at the task he had set for himself. The thick stone that lay on the ground was over five feet long and weighed hundreds of pounds. No man could possibly move this stone unless the gods were with him.

He prayed during the night, and in the morning he felt powerful. He watched other men strain and push against the stone. It did not move.

Then it was Kamehameha's turn. He walked to the mighty rock and looked at it from all sides. The crowd gathered around him. He reached out and touched the stone and felt a wave of energy pass through his body. Drawing a deep breath, he bent his knees and pressed against his silent opponent. Using all his weight and muscles, he heaved his body into the boulder. The boulder shifted slightly. He grasped the sides and felt an edge of the great lava rock lift off the ground. The people all around him gasped in amazement.

Now, using his last remaining power, he strained with a mighty effort. His teeth clenched and his muscles bulged as he gave a final shove. The great Naha Stone turned over!

Before the high chiefs, *kahunas*, warriors, and commoners, Kamehameha had done the impossible. Many threw themselves face down on the dusty ground to honor him. A *kahuna* at the time of Kamehameha's birth had said a child would be born who would rise to conquer rival chiefs. The Naha Stone's legend promised that he who could conquer the stone would conquer the islands.

Kamehameha would be king.

C H A P T E R 5

WARRIOR

Kamehameha had his first chance for battle when he was seventeen. His uncle, Kalaniʻōpuʻu, decided to invade Maui to fight the great chief Kahekili. Now at last Kamehameha would test his skills and years of warrior training.

"I'm ready," he said to himself, knotting his muscles and slashing the air with his spear. "I hope I am chosen to go. I will battle Kahekili myself," he said, not realizing he might be speaking of his own father.

Kalaniʻōpuʻu announced the chiefs and warriors who would accompany him. Kamehameha waited anxiously. He heard the name of his teacher and friend, Kekūhaupiʻo, and then, elated,

he heard his own name called. They were assigned to the same canoe.

This was Kamehameha's first trip away from the island. He felt the surge of the sea and the spray upon his face as the canoes neared Maui. He eagerly watched the shore, impatient to land.

He turned to Kekūhaupi'o in the canoe and grinned. "Well, my friend, now I will learn how well you have taught me."

The older warrior laughed. "I see you are excited to wage your first battle. Do not be too bold, or it may be your last."

The canoes landed on the beach as the morning sun shone on the green mountains. The men leapt from the canoes armed with their spears and clubs.

Kahekili's forces were waiting. They advanced toward the invaders, hurling rocks of black lava from their slings.

The sun rose higher as the battle moved away from the beach toward the hills. Kamehameha thrust his spear and swung his club as one warrior after another charged him. Sweat shone on his broad back, and his muscles rippled as he fought in the day's heat. He was hot and thirsty, but he never once stopped to think about his discomfort. He was looking for Kahekili, the great warrior chief of Maui. He longed to fight him.

The battle was not going well, however. Before Kamehameha could find the enemy chief, Kalani'ōpu'u, who had lost many of his men to Kahekili's forces, called to his remaining warriors to return to their canoes.

By now the sun was spilling its long, amber rays of late afternoon, and the shadows of the warriors lengthened. Kamehameha headed down the mountain searching for Kekūhaupi'o. They had fought side by side earlier but had become separated. Kamehameha could not find his friend anywhere among the retreating men, and finally he turned back toward the mountain. He would not leave Maui without Kekūhaupiʻo.

Then he saw him. Kekūhaupiʻo had fallen, his legs entangled in the sweet potato vines that laced the mountain fields. He was valiantly warding off the clubs of his enemies who were attacking him mercilessly. But he was outnumbered and trapped by the green vines.

Kamehameha ran to his fallen friend. With a roar, he hurled himself against the attackers. The surprised warriors of Kahekili fled from this terrible onslaught. He hacked at the vines and freed his comrade. They hurried together down the mountain and reached the shore as the last canoes were pulling away from the beach.

Gasping for breath, Kekūhaupiʻo clasped Kamehameha about the shoulders as their canoe headed home to Hawaiʻi. The sky and sea reddened with sunset. "I taught you well," he said. "You saved my life."

Though the battle was lost, Kamehameha proved that he had grown into a warrior to be feared.

CHAPTER 6

FLOATING ISLANDS
AND FIRE-STICKS

*T*hree years later, in November 1778, Kamehameha returned to Maui to the rocky shore of Hāna with his uncle, Kalani'ōpu'u. One day, as he stood on the beach looking out toward the sea, his dark eyes widened.

"Uncle!" He grasped the chief's arm, "Look!"

Like two giant birds, the ships sailed by, fluttering their white wings.

"What are they, Uncle?"

"They are the ships I have been telling you about of the white

god who came once before. They have sticks that make fire and large, round stones that give a loud sound when they are thrown over the side. This god, some say, is Lono, because of the white banners on his ship, which are like those of Lono. But he says his name is Captain Cook, and he comes from a land across the ocean."

As the two ships sailed past Hāna, Kamehameha watched them intently.

"How powerful I would be if I had ships like that," he thought to himself, holding his feathered cape tightly about him. "They are like floating islands on the sea."

The next day he rode out in a canoe to visit the ships. He eyed the strangers warily.

"Look how pale their skin is," he commented to his uncle. "They must not live in the sun as we do. How strange their clothes are. They are not made from feathers or *kapa*. They fit around their limbs like a second skin."

He watched Captain Cook from a distance. The captain seemed very stern, and he held himself proudly. Kamehameha could see that he was a very important man. But he was not sure that the captain was a god, as some people thought.

The captain looked at Kamehameha, also, and nodded as his lieutenant said to him, "He has as savage a face as I've ever seen."

Kamehameha studied the metal nails and tools on board the ships, as well as the metal guns that glinted in the sun. His tools and weapons were made from wood, bone, and shell. He had never seen metal before.

He stayed on board overnight, watching the ways of these strange new people, and then a canoe arrived to return him to the king's camp at Hāna. He was quiet and thoughtful for several days.

When the king and his court returned to Hawaiʻi in January, Captain Cook's ships, the *Resolution* and the *Discovery,* had arrived in Kealakekua Bay, where they dropped anchor.

"Uncle," Kamehameha said to Kalaniʻōpuʻu, "if we had sticks like the white man has that make fire, we could win our battles against Kahekili."

Captain Cook remained in Hawaiʻi refitting his ships and getting ready for the long voyage north. He was on a mission to search for the fabled Northwest Passage, a sea route above North America that would connect the Pacific and Atlantic Oceans.

Kamehameha visited the ships often, trying to learn as much as possible. He admired the iron daggers made by the blacksmiths and acquired nine of them. He gave them hogs, bananas, and breadfruit in return.

Finally, the Europeans were ready to sail, and the villagers turned out to see them on their way.

Kalaniʻōpuʻu said to Kamehameha, "It is time they left. They have used up a lot of our pigs, vegetables, and fish, and they have taken up our people's time."

Kamehameha was sorry he couldn't get any of the crew to give him a gun.

After the ships sailed, the king put the bay under a *kapu* to provide time for replenishment. All was quiet and peaceful. Then, suddenly, Captain Cook and his ships returned.

One of the masts had broken as the ships rounded the northern point of the island. They had to come back to Kealakekua Bay for repairs.

The villagers were not happy to see them return and did not provide the cheerful welcome they had in the past. They were quiet and watchful, and the sailors felt wary, too.

Somebody stole a boat from one of the ships. The British fired upon some villagers, and Kamehameha was hit with flying rocks from the guns' impact. Tensions rose. Captain Cook, angry over the stolen boat, went ashore with two boatloads of men, determined to take Kalani'ōpu'u hostage until the boat was returned. The king's wives and advisors feared for his life and begged him not to go.

The villagers became more uneasy and began moving about. Suddenly, the sound of gunfire from one of the ships echoed across the bay.

With a shout, a man standing near Captain Cook attacked him with a dagger. Cook fired his gun. The men in the boats and those on shore opened fire. Cook turned to wave the boats in and was hit on the head with a club. Then another warrior stabbed him in the back. Kamehameha looked on in shock as the wounded captain fell with a groan into the shallow water and died.

The Hawaiians began to attack all the Britishers around them. A lieutenant hastily called the men back to their ships, leaving the body of their dead captain on the rocky beach.

Kamehameha had admired Captain Cook and was dismayed that he had been killed. When the body of Captain Cook was divided among several chiefs, according to Hawaiian custom, Kamehameha received the hair. The Hawaiians believed that acquiring parts of an important man's body could increase a person's *mana*.

Kamehameha sent hogs to the ships to help supply them for

their sad journey. He watched as the ships left Kealakekua Bay and thought about all he had learned during the white men's stay. He had seen their guns and cannons, and he knew that, if he had the opportunity, future wars would be fought in a different way from the past.

WAR AND LOVE

*M*eanwhile, Kamehameha's uncle, Kalani'ōpu'u, was growing old. He gathered his chiefs together at a temple among the ferns and waterfalls of Waipi'o Valley.

"The time has come to name my heirs," he announced, "for I shall soon pass from this life. Kiwala'ō, my son, you will inherit my kingdom. And to you, Kamehameha, my dear nephew, I give the custody of the war god, Kūkā'ilimoku." He handed Kamehameha the image of the god. It was over two feet tall and covered with feathers, with glaring eyes made of shell and a ferocious mouth made of ninety-four dogs' teeth.

The two rival cousins, Kiwala'ō and Kamehameha, stared at each other as Kamehameha accepted the war god.

Soon Kalaniʻōpuʻu died, and several chiefs convinced Kamehameha to help them wage war against Kiwalaʻō and Kiwalaʻō's brother, Keōua.

Kamehameha's ally, Keʻeaumoku, fell during the battle, entangled by his own spear, and was stabbed with a dagger. He lay bleeding not far from Kiwalaʻō, who had been felled by a sling stone. With his strength ebbing, Keʻeaumoku crawled to Kiwalaʻō and cut his throat with a dagger edged with sharks' teeth. Kiwalaʻō bled to death.

Keʻeaumoku, who recovered from his wounds, had fulfilled the first part of a prophecy. Once long ago, when Keʻeaumoku lived in Hāna, a traveler came from over the mountains. A prophet and composer of chants, he sat for hours and dreamed, and then he suddenly began to chant. In a singsong voice, he spoke to Keʻeaumoku:

"You will become a slayer of princes and a maker of kings. Your daughter will become the wife of a king."

Now, with Kiwalaʻō's death, Keʻeaumoku had become the slayer of a prince. Whom would he help to make a king? And whom would his daughter marry?

One evening, Keʻeaumoku's daughter accompanied him in the village. When Kamehameha saw her, he stared at her with admiration. She was nearly as tall as he and carried herself proudly.

"My father tells me you are a great warrior," she said to him. The evening torches had been lit, and the flames cast shadows across her face as she spoke. Drumbeats began pulsing through the night air as the villagers gathered.

"Who are you?" he asked.

"I am Kaʻahumanu, daughter of Keʻeaumoku."

They began to spend time together and often rode the waves on *koa* boards. She was as skilled a surfer as he, and strong. They paddled the long, heavy boards out past the waves, then, turning, raced to catch the cresting curl of water.

Soon, Kamehameha went to Keʻeaumoku and told him, "I want to marry your daughter."

"My friend," Keʻeaumoku responded, "nothing would please me more. She is very beautiful and very smart. She will make you happy, and she will help you in your quest for power."

Kamehameha and the spirited, proud Kaʻahumanu were married in a simple ceremony and began their life together.

Now that Kaʻahumanu was Kamehameha's wife, would the rest of the prophecy come true—that she would be the wife of a king?

KING OF HAWAI'I

Now that the Hawaiian Islands had been discovered by the outside world, the first American and English traders began to arrive on their way to China and back. They brought many wonderful treasures with them, such as silk, clothes, and furniture. But most important to Kamehameha were the guns and cannon they carried on their ships. He wanted them for himself. His chance came when Kaiana, a tall chief from Kaua'i, came to Hawai'i. He had sailed to China, and the captain of the ship had given him many presents, including muskets and ammunition.

"Kaiana," Kamehameha clapped him on the shoulder, "if you

will stay here and help me get guns, I will give you land and make you a general among my warriors."

Kaiana answered, "That is a good offer. I accept."

Kaiana persuaded the captain to supply Kamehameha not only with hand-held guns but also with a swivel gun, which Kamehameha had mounted on a double canoe.

Kamehameha was pleased with his new friend, little suspecting Kaiana would one day betray him in both love and war.

Now, with his new weapons, he needed the skills of Western sailors to operate and care for them properly. He soon obtained two English seamen. Isaac Davis had been the only survivor of an attack by a Kona chief against the *Fair American*. Kamehameha seized the ship from this chief and took Isaac Davis into his care. At the same time, John Young, the boatswain of the *Eleanora*, had come ashore for supplies. Kamehameha kept him from returning to his ship, and the *Eleanora* sailed away.

In addition to guns, ammunition, and a swivel gun on a canoe, Kamehameha now also had a sailing ship and its cannon. And now he also had two sailors to handle them. He gave the two men land, wives, and positions of power in his court.

They tried to escape.

"This isn't our kind of life," John Young protested when they were captured and brought back to Kamehameha, who was very angry.

"If you ever try to leave again," Kamehameha thundered, "I'll kill you."

The two men did not try to run away a second time.

Kamehameha decided to attack Maui. Kahekili was on O'ahu and had left Maui in charge of his son, Kalanikūpule. Kahekili was still the most powerful chief of all the islands, and Kamehameha had not yet fought this warrior who, unknown to him, was said to be his father. Now he prepared himself to fight Kalanikūpule, who—if Kahekili was Kamehameha's father—was Kamehameha's own half-brother.

Kamehameha drove his war canoes up on the sands of Maui. He marched against the enemy and pushed them into the steep, narrow valley of 'Īao. Isaac Davis and John Young manned the cannon, and the air was filled with clouds of smoke and the sound of thunder. The waters of the river filled with bodies, and the battle was called Kepaniwai, the Damming of the Waters.

Kalanikūpule escaped over the mountains to his canoe and fled to his father. Kamehameha sent his messenger to Kahekili, carrying two stones. The white stone was for peace, and the black stone was for war. Kahekili sent the messenger back to Kamehameha, telling him, "Go back and tell Kamehameha to return to Hawai'i, and when the black *kapa* covers Kahekili and the black pig rests at his nose," meaning that he would then be dead, "then is the time to cast stones."

Kamehameha did return to Hawai'i, not because of this message, but because of war. His cousin Keōua, who controlled a large section of the island, was destroying taro patches, fish-ponds, and villages belonging to Kamehameha.

Kamehameha rushed back to Hawai'i to fight. After two battles, Keōua and his forces retreated. As they scrambled past the volcanic crater of Kīlauea, a sudden eruption enveloped them. Many were killed by the poisonous gasses and volcanic ash. Footprints of the dying warriors can still be seen, preserved in the petrified earth.

According to legend, Pele, the goddess of fire, lives in Halema'uma'u, the fire pit within Kīlauea Crater. Was this eruption an omen that the goddess favored Kamehameha? If Pele was on his side, who would dare to oppose him?

But Kamehameha also needed the help of the war god, Kūkā'ilimoku, according to a *kahuna* who told Kamehameha that he must build a new *heiau* to gain the god's support.

Kamehameha chose a site on the northwest coast of the island. But the building of the temple was interrupted when Kahekili challenged Kamehameha to a sea battle. The sea turned red with blood, and the battle was known as *Kepūwaha'ula'ula*, the Battle of the Red-Mouthed Gun. However, neither side won. Kahekili went back to Maui, and Kamehameha returned to complete his *heiau*.

This was Kahekili's last battle and the last time he would ever encounter Kamehameha. It is possible that Kahekili thought that Kamehameha was his son, but at that time, Kamehameha was not aware of any relationship.

In 1791, the *heiau*, Pu'ukoholā, was finally finished, and Kamehameha invited Keōua to visit him there. Keōua arrived, clad in his feather cape and helmet, his double canoe accompanied by twenty-six other canoes filled with warriors. When his canoe beached, he called, "Here I am." Kamehameha, also in his feather cloak and helmet, called back, "Stand up and come forward that we may greet each other."

As the tense crowd gathered around, Keōua stepped onto the shore. Ke'eaumoku emerged from the crowd, raised his spear, and hurled it at Keōua. The spear pierced Keōua's chest, and he died. As with Keōua's brother, Kiwala'ō, Ke'eaumoku had again fulfilled the prophecy that he was a "slayer of princes."

Keōua's body was offered to the war god on the altar of the new *heiau*. Kamehameha was now the king of the island of Hawai'i.

CHAPTER 9

A FRIEND FROM
ACROSS THE SEA

Kamehameha had gained the first step in the drive for conquest. He was the ruler of the island of Hawai'i. He farmed his lands, traded with the foreigners, and enjoyed a period of peace from 1792 to 1794.

During this time, he became close friends with George Vancouver, who had once been a seaman on Captain Cook's crew. Now, thirteen years later, Vancouver commanded his own ships, the *Chatham* and the *Discovery*, and had returned to the islands.

CHAPTER 9

"His riper years," Vancouver wrote of Kamehameha, "had softened that stern ferocity which his younger years had exhibited."

He praised Kamehameha's cheerfulness and generosity, and he admired his skill. He once spoke of a time during a contest when Kamehameha had six spears thrown at him at the same time. He sidestepped two, parried the rest, and was not struck.

Vancouver invited Ka'ahumanu and Kamehameha to sail along the Kona coast with him. He found Ka'ahumanu one of the finest women he had met in the islands, and he was touched by Kamehameha and Ka'ahumanu's affection for each other.

He was not happy when, later, the couple separated. Kamehameha had become very angry because Ka'ahumanu had flirted with the handsome Kaiana. At the same time, Ka'ahumanu was upset because Kamehameha was thinking of taking another wife, Keōpūolani, who ranked higher than she did. Ka'ahumanu left Kamehameha and went home to live with her parents.

One day Vancouver invited Ka'ahumanu to visit him on his ship. He arranged to have Kamehameha come on board a little later, as though by chance. She arrived and was escorted to the captain's lounge. Suddenly Kamehameha appeared before her. She looked at him in astonishment, and then, with a sob, she flung herself into his arms.

"Vancouver," Kamehameha smiled through tears, "thank you, my friend, for bringing us together again."

Vancouver was a man of peace and was happy to have brought harmony back to the lives of his friends. He also sought harmony among the chiefs. When Kamehameha wanted guns and cannon from him, he refused because he did not want to encourage war. Instead, he gave Kamehameha cattle, sheep, goats, geese, grapevines, and orange trees. Kamehameha was delighted with the cattle, marveling at their size. He called them "large hogs" and watched eagerly as they were loaded from the ships onto large canoes to come ashore.

He and Vancouver exchanged gifts of clothing. He gave Vancouver four feathered helmets, and Vancouver presented him with a scarlet English cloak, edged with lace and tied with blue satin ribbons. Vancouver also arranged to rig a double canoe for Kamehameha with a full suit of canvas sails and a Union Jack, the flag of Great Britain. Later, he ordered a ship built for Kamehameha, a thirty-six-foot sloop, the *Britannia*. Kamehameha spent hours watching the building of this, his very own sailing ship.

Vancouver and Kamehameha spoke together many times about politics and religion. One day Vancouver said, "Your gods are not real. They are only images of feathers and dog's teeth. You must cast them aside and abide by the true God."

Kamehameha thought a while and then replied, "My friend, you and my *kahuna* will climb the mountain and hurl yourselves from the cliff. If your god saves you, I will know that yours is the true god, and I will give up my gods."

Vancouver had no answer for this, as he did not want to jump off a cliff to prove his faith.

As for politics, Vancouver told Kamehameha he would be wise to put his island under the protection of Great Britain. Kamehameha agreed, and, on February 25, 1794, aboard the *Discovery*, Kamehameha announced that he and his people were now subjects of Great Britain. The British flag was raised on shore, and a salute was fired. This announcement was never recognized by the British government, but for years Kamehameha considered Hawai'i to be under the protection of Great Britain.

Vancouver left the islands for the last time to return to England in March 1794. The two friends embraced and said farewell. Kamehameha stood on the beach and sadly watched his friend's ship sail away forever.

Unknowingly, he was also saying farewell to the brief time of peace in the islands.

CONQUEST

As Vancouver sailed away, Kahekili lay ill in Waikīkī. He died in the spring. Now no great warrior chief lived who could challenge Kamehameha. Even Kahekili's son, Kalanikūpule, had run from him on Maui.

Kamehameha gathered his chiefs together. Kalanikūpule was causing trouble, he told them. Kalanikūpule killed his uncle, Kāʻeo, using guns and sailors from the English ships. Then he turned on the English and captured their ships, killing the captain. He was sailing to Hawaiʻi to attack Kamehameha when the English got their ships back and sent Kalanikūpule to shore in a canoe.

Kamehameha amassed his war canoes. With Kaiana, Keʻeau-moku, and his other chiefs, he swept across Maui and Molokaʻi with sixteen thousand men. The two islands and Lānaʻi quickly fell under his control. He traveled on to Oʻahu and beached his canoes along the shore from Waikīkī to Waiʻalae.

Kamehameha stepped ashore and gazed across the plains toward the mountains. Somewhere Kalanikūpule was waiting for him, forewarned by Kaiana. During the night, while crossing the Molokaʻi Channel, treacherous Kaiana had deserted. Taking many canoes with him, he slipped away from the fleet and landed on Oʻahu to join Kalanikūpule.

Kamehameha and Kaiana had not been friends since Kaiana had tried to steal Kaʻahumanu away from Kamehameha. They argued often over Kaiana's demands for more power. But Kamehameha had not believed the rift was so great that Kaiana would betray him. He gripped his spear angrily and said to himself, "Now I will have to fight twice as hard to win."

He watched with satisfaction as John Young and Isaac Davis unloaded the cannon from the boat. Many of his men had muskets, ammunition, and steel cutlasses. The others carried their spears, war clubs, and daggers. He held a council with Keʻeaumoku and his other chiefs and said, "We will march toward the valley and corner them against the mountains."

They began their march across the plains toward the narrow green valley, which was deeply carved by the Nuʻuanu Stream. There, Kalanikūpule made his stand on the steep slope of the valley entrance. The battle mounted as the long spears flew and clubs cracked. Guns thundered between the valley walls.

Kamehameha relentlessly drove forward, pushing the enemy deeper into the valley. Hemmed in on either side by the brood-

ing mountains, he fought his way toward the brink of the
Nuʻuanu Pali. Beyond lay the fearsome drop over the cliffs.

Suddenly Kaiana appeared among his warriors and glared
defiantly at Kamehameha. Kamehameha turned to John Young,
who had the cannon, and yelled, "Fire! Kill the traitor!" The
cannonball roared through the air and hurled into Kaiana with
a fatal blow. His men became alarmed when they saw their
leader die, and they fled in panic.

Kamehameha pressed forward as Kalanikūpule and Kaiana's remaining forces struggled to get out of the way. Though
some hid and others scrambled over the mountains, many were
pushed to the edge of the Pali. With Kamehameha and his warriors right behind them, they either jumped or were forced over
the cliff to their deaths on the jagged rocks far below.

Kalanikūpule, who was wounded, ran away. Kamehameha's
men dragged him from his hiding place in an old *heiau* and sac-
rificed him to the war god. Bones from his body were taken to
make Kamehameha a new *kāhili*, a feather staff, which was the
symbol of power and divinity.

The battle for Oʻahu was ended and Kamehameha had now
conquered all of the islands, except for Kauaʻi and its neighbor,
Niʻihau. He looked across the mountains toward the sea and
thought of the time years ago when as a young boy he had stood
on another mountain and dreamed of this moment.

THE CAMPAIGN

FOR KAUA'I

Kamehameha now prepared to move on to Kaua'i. In the spring of 1796, he prayed to his war god at a temple on the west of O'ahu and offered human sacrifices to the fierce glaring image. Then, in the middle of the night, with his great fleet of war canoes, he set out for Kaua'i. But as the canoes crossed the channel, a wild wind blew and whipped the sea into stormy waves. Many of the canoes overturned or filled with water and Kamehameha was forced to return.

"My god protected me," he said. "I am alive. But he is telling

me I must wait for another time." Giving up the invasion, Kamehameha returned to the island of Hawai'i.

He took another wife, the highborn Keōpūolani, and, in 1797, she gave birth to Kamehameha's first royal son, Liholiho.

Though he was content on Hawai'i with his new family life, the thought of Kaua'i continued to nag at Kamehameha. For five years he had his workers build a new fleet of canoes. Double-hulled and larger than regular canoes, they were broad and deep, with covered platforms. Some were rigged with sails. Eight hundred of these were built, capable of carrying several thousand warriors. At the same time, Kamehameha's carpenters were building him new sailing ships upon which he mounted cannon.

Kamehameha wanted all of the islands under his control. Kaumuali'i, the young king of Kaua'i, anxiously watched Kamehameha's moves.

In 1802, Kamehameha moved his new fleet to Maui, where he stayed for a year while preparing for a new invasion of Kaua'i. During this time on Maui, in the shadow of the mountains where he had once long ago fought in a battle against the mighty Kahekili, he at last learned the rumor of his birth. An old warrior, who had been one of his chief counselors all his life, became ill and was dying. He called Kamehameha to his side and bid him good-bye.

"I have been guarding this secret since your birth," he said, his voice raspy with exertion. "But now I must tell you who you really are."

"What do you mean, who I really am? I am Kamehameha!"

"Yes, my dear friend. You are Kamehameha. But you are

not the son of Keōua," he whispered. "Kahekili was your true father."

Thunderstruck, Kamehameha stared at him and shook his head unbelievingly. If this were true, his own father had been his greatest rival. In the battles where they had fought against each other, Kamehameha had fought to kill. That would also mean that Kalanikūpule was his half-brother whom he had killed at the Battle of Nuʻuanu.

Kamehameha sat for a long time by the side of the old man's body and thought about this possibility and of the *mana* that would be his because of Kahekili's greatness. Was this why he had always felt so invincible? He spent a few days thinking, and then he decided, "If he were my father, he would want me to continue my quest. I shall unite the islands."

He left Maui soon after and moved his fleet to Oʻahu. He had sent a message to Kaumualiʻi, urging Kaumualiʻi to accept him as his king. When Kaumualiʻi did not respond, Kamehameha again readied for invasion.

But once again, Kamehameha was prevented from crossing the Kauaʻi Channel. A terrible disease broke out on Oʻahu and quickly spread among the people. Many died in agony. Kamehameha himself became very ill. He recovered, but no amount of prayers, offerings, or sacrifices to the gods could end the dread epidemic until it had run its course. Countless died, including Kamehameha's most important chiefs. His greatest chief, Keʻeaumoku, the "maker of kings," was among them.

Heartsick, Kamehameha gave up his plans to invade Kauaʻi for the second time. The warriors buried their dead, and the great fleet of canoes lay on the sands and slowly rotted in the sun.

CHAPTER 12

KING OF ALL
THE ISLANDS

Kamehameha decided to remain on O'ahu. The harbor there was ideal for trading ships, and a booming business began to develop around the busy port of Honolulu. He did not forget Kaua'i, however, and still tried to bring the island under his rule. Finally he sent a message to the king of Kaua'i, Kaumuali'i, saying there would be no war if only Kaumuali'i would pay him yearly taxes. The Kaua'i king could still control his island as long as he was willing to pay homage to Kamehameha

▼▼▼▼▼▼▼▼▼▼▼▼▼▼▼▼▼▼

and accept his leadership. Kaumuali'i agreed to this, but Kamehameha insisted that he come to O'ahu and make the agreement in person.

Kaumuali'i was not eager to make the trip. He remembered the fate of Kamehameha's cousin, who had come in friendship and had been killed before Kamehameha's eyes.

Captain Nathan Winship, an American trader, wanted to see peace between the two. He persuaded the Kaua'i chief to make the journey and brought him to O'ahu on his ship, the *Albatross*.

As the *Albatross* approached the harbor, Kamehameha went to meet it with a fleet of canoes. He came on board, and at last the two chiefs met face-to-face in their long cloaks and helmets.

Kaumuali'i greeted Kamehameha by saying, "Here I am. Is it face up or face down?" This meant, "Do I live or die?"

Kamehameha responded, "There will be no death. Give me your hand."

The two then agreed that Kaumuali'i would continue to rule over Kaua'i, but that Kaumuali'i would pay taxes to Kamehameha and accept him as the king of all the islands.

Kaumuali'i said, "Now we have met and agreed. I shall return to Kaua'i."

Kamehameha replied, "No, let us land. I have planned a celebration."

During the feast, some of the chiefs attempted to poison Kaumuali'i. Warned by Isaac Davis, Kaumuali'i quickly left O'ahu with Captain Winship and returned safely to Kaua'i.

Isaac Davis died mysteriously soon after, possibly poisoned by these same chiefs in revenge for spoiling their plot.

However, the question of Kaua'i was now settled, and Kamehameha sent off another letter to King George III of Great Britain, announcing that Kamehameha now controlled all of the Hawaiian Islands, including Kaua'i. With the letter, he sent King George a feather cloak. In return, he received a gold-laced, cocked hat and a red uniform coat.

Kamehameha could at last lay down his gun and his spear. By April 1810, he had united the islands.

KAMEHAMEHA'S RULE

The war years were over. Kamehameha put away his weapons and said, "Now we will have prosperity. What was the reason for all these years of strife if not to bring together a peaceful and rich kingdom that we may all enjoy? The fields are barren. We must begin by replenishing the land."

Along the shore and into the valley he went, planting crops, digging ditches to water the land, and building ponds to keep fish. He made his home in Honolulu because the busy harbor there was good for trade. He enjoyed the foreigners and their worldly possessions and believed that wealth for his kingdom was linked by commerce with other lands.

When ships entered the harbor, Kamehameha directed them to anchorage, standing proudly in his seventy-five-foot double canoe manned by a hundred men. Sometimes he greeted his visitors in his feather cloak and helmet; other times he wore a British regimental uniform and carried a sword.

Trade developed swiftly. Though he could neither read nor write, Kamehameha learned to speak English and understood the weights and measures used in trade.

He soon had storehouses filled with silk, silver, and china. Sandalwood became the most sought-after product in the islands, and Kamehameha, realizing its value, took complete control over it. This fragrant wood grew in the mountains, where it was cut down and hauled to the sea to be sent on sailing ships to Canton.

Though Kamehameha attended carefully to the business of trade and the visiting foreigners, he spent much of his time now farming his plantations. Some days he rode his horse to survey the land.

"Bring me my horse," he commanded. Soon a spirited, prancing horse was led to him by one of his men.

"Ah, Kawaiolaloa, you are ready for another adventure, I see." Kamehameha patted the horse fondly. Kawaiolaloa had been given to him by an American sea captain, William Shaler, who had brought several horses to the islands in 1803. Kamehameha learned to ride easily and became a graceful horseman.

Children gathered around. "The king rides today," they whispered to one another, peeking over the walls to see the great beast that would carry their king on its back. Kamehameha mounted the horse, straddled its glistening bare back, took the reins in his hands, and rode through the village. Along the paths, the villagers lined up to watch their king leave to visit his country property.

The children fell into step behind Kawaiolaloa and followed as Kamehameha rode up through the narrow green valley of Nuʻuanu, winding along the mountainsides where he once had slain his enemies. The procession moved along to Mānoa Valley and across the plains to the sea at Waikīkī, where Kamehameha came often to surf on his long *koa* board. Then, turning homeward, he led Kawaiolaloa along the sea's edge back to his court at the harbor, the dusty, laughing children tumbling behind.

"The land breathes again," he told his followers. "The vines of the sweet potatoes tangle in the fields, and the leaves of the taro are rich and green. Fish jump in the ponds. Trade is good at the harbor and on the ships of the foreigners. But now I am homesick for the land of my childhood. I am becoming old and long for the simpler life of my earlier years." He turned to his trusted chiefs and advisors. "I leave this island in your charge."

In 1812, he put his family and members of his court aboard two sailing ships and returned to Kailua-Kona on the island of Hawaiʻi.

THE SETTLED YEARS

The Kona coast was a bleak land. The volcano that rose behind Kailua had erupted in 1801. Burning lava had covered the ground all the way to the sea and twenty miles along the coast. The eruption had destroyed stone walls, trees, villages, and fishponds. Offerings of live hogs were tossed into the burning rivers of lava, but the molten flow still poured down the mountain.

Kamehameha, who had been there at the time of the eruption, finally went to the hurtling lava. With his chiefs and priests he prayed to Pele to stop the flow. The flow continued. A *kahuna* said, "Only that which is most sacred will appease her. You must offer something of yourself, my king." Kamehameha cut

off several pieces of his hair and threw them into the fire. The eruption ceased. Pele was calm again. She still favored Kamehameha.

Now, eleven years later, Kamehameha was back in Kona to stay. He fished and surfed and spent many hours tending the black, hostile ground. He worked in his garden and carried rocks to build new *heiau*. In spite of his involvement with the outside world, Kamehameha kept the old religion of his ancestors. The *kapu* system, he felt, was the right one to live by.

"My religion," he claimed, "cannot be bad because it teaches me to do no wrong." He ordered his people to live in peace and safety.

Years before, he had leapt from a canoe to attack some fishermen on the beach. He slipped and caught his foot in a lava crevice. While he was helpless, a fisherman hit him on the head with a paddle. He hit him so hard that the paddle splintered. The fisherman was later caught and brought to Kamehameha to be punished. But Kamehameha said, "You may go free. I had no right to attack you. You were innocent." As a result of this incident, Kamehameha, now as the king and maker of laws, proclaimed the "Law of the Splintered Paddle" that said, "Let the aged, men, women, and little children lie down in safety on the road. Disobey this and die."

Now at last Kamehameha had time to spend with his family. He announced that his son Liholiho would be the heir to the kingdom, and he spent many hours with his son teaching him the ways of government. Though his wife Ka'ahumanu had no children of her own, she was his most powerful wife and had a strong hand in raising Liholiho. Keōpūolani was the highest ranking of Kamehameha's wives. Though she did not live with

Kamehameha and was allowed other husbands, she was the mother of his heirs. She and Kamehameha had two more children. A son, Kauikeaouli, was born in 1814, and a daughter, Nāhiʻenaʻena, in 1815.

One day while a Russian ship was anchored offshore, the ship's artist, Choris, came to the king's house to paint a portrait. Kamehameha was sitting outside wearing a red *malo* and a black *kapa* cape, with a straw hat on his head. When he saw that Choris was going to paint his picture, he stood up and commanded, "Wait!" He soon returned wearing a shirt, red vest, and blue sailor pants. The portrait shows Kamehameha with a strong face, full lips, broad nose, and short gray hair.

For all his ability to conquer and rule his people and to handle foreign powers, Kamehameha had a simple, wondering view of the world. Once a foreigner tried to explain that the earth was round. The king thought about this for a long time. Then he took a plate and put a biscuit on it, with another smaller piece on top. He held up the plate. "Here is the earth," he said, holding the plate. "The biscuit is Hawaiʻi and the small piece is I." He turned the plate upside down so that everything fell on the ground. Gravity was not an idea he could understand.

He was wise in the ways of war and government, however, and ruled his domains carefully until the end of his life. His people said of him: "He is a father to the fatherless, a savior to the old and the weak, a farmer, a fisherman, and a provider for the needy."

THE FINAL DAYS

The end came on May 8, 1819. Francisco de Paula Marin, a Spaniard who had some knowledge of medicine, was sent for from Honolulu to cure the king. When he arrived in Kailua, the king was very ill. Kamehameha was taken back and forth from the sleeping house to the eating house. He could eat only a little *poi* as he gasped for breath. His followers built a *heiau* to the war god and asked that a human sacrifice be made that the king might live. But the king refused, saying that all men were to be saved for the next king, his son Liholiho.

The great king lay dying, surrounded by his chiefs, his wives, his children, and his good friends, John Young and Marin. They said, "Lay upon us your last command."

Kamehameha whispered hoarsely, "Move on in my good way ..." Whatever he meant to say was lost. He could speak no more.

The tides rose and brimmed with 'āweoweo fish, a sign of death. Kamehameha was dead.

His followers went into deep mourning. They wailed and clamored, knocking out their teeth and cutting off their hair. Some tattooed themselves with the name of their leader and the date of his death.

According to the custom of burial for kings, Kamehameha's bones were secretly buried to protect his *mana*. A trusted chief hid them in a cave overlooking the sea. It is said, "Only the stars of the heavens know the resting place of Kamehameha."

Kamehameha the Great, a strong warrior and a dedicated king, had fulfilled the prophecy of his birth. He united the Hawaiian Islands under one rule, and the kingdom of Hawai'i lasted for nearly a century.

To this day, Kamehameha is Hawai'i's greatest hero. Every year in June, there is a special holiday in honor of him. This day is called "Kamehameha Day" and is highlighted with a big parade. A nuclear submarine was named *Kamehameha*, honoring him as a great American statesman. His statue stands in front of Ali'iōlani Hale, across from Iolani Palace, and in North Kohala. A replica of this statue has been placed in Statuary Hall in the Capitol Building in Washington, D.C.

Kamehameha's feathered cloak, his *kāhili*, and his war god, Kū, are in the Bishop Museum in Honolulu.

N O T E S

Further information about the sources mentioned below appears in the Bibliography.

Birth Date

Because Kamehameha was born before Hawai'i's recorded history, many of the details of his birth will never be known. There are several reputable sources for the date of his birth, and most estimates place it between 1736 and 1761. The year 1758 is considered by many to be the most likely for several reasons. This date is implied by one of the earliest sources, Francisco de Paula Marin, who was at Kamehameha's deathbed in 1819 and claimed he died at the age of 60.5. Also, a great star was said to blaze overhead at the time of his birth. Halley's Comet was in the sky at the time of 'Ikuwā, in 1758.

For further discussion, see "Report to the Hawaiian Historical Society by its Trustees Concerning the Birth Date of Kamehameha I and Kamehameha Day Celebrations," Makemson, Stokes, and Kuykendall.

Birthplace

Several theories exist as to why Keku'iapoiwa was in northern Kohala at the time of Kamehameha's birth. One is that she was fleeing from Alapa'i, the jealous chief of the island of Hawai'i, because he had ordered newborn babies killed due to a prophecy. The prophecy was that a baby would be born who would one day rise to slay his rivals and become the ruler. In another theory, Alapa'i was preparing to invade Maui and had traveled to the north end of Hawai'i with his court as a staging area for the attack, and the baby disappeared under mysterious circumstances. A third theory is that Alapa'i and his court were living in Kohala at the time. Finally, a fourth theory is simply that Keku'iapoiwa had come there for the express purpose of giving birth at a special birthing place.

Since no one account seems to me more verifiable than another, I don't

67

state precisely why Kekuʻiapoiwa was in Kohala, but she indeed was there. Several exact locations in north Kohala have been listed, and though Kokoiki was the most likely, I merely state that it was the northern tip of Hawaiʻi.

As to whether Alapaʻi intended to have the baby killed, many accounts seem to support this theory.

For further discussion, see Kamakau, Starbuck, Judd, and Alexander.

Birth Father

The third mystery of Kamehameha's birth is his parentage. Kekuʻiapoiwa was undoubtedly his mother. She was married to the chief Keōua, who is legally considered to be his father. However, even at the time of Kamehameha's birth, it was rumored that his father was none other than Kahekili, the great warrior chief of Maui. Kekuʻiapoiwa visited his court after her marriage to Keōua and gave birth within the next nine months. Some historians even claim that double paternity was considered an honor, as it conferred a double line of chief descent and therefore doubled the *mana* of the child (see Kamakau). However, since neither man's paternity can be verified, this version is suggested only as a possibility.

For further discussion, see Dibble, Judd, Kamakau, Starbuck, Alexander, and Jarves.

Conversations

I have tried to keep to conversation that has been quoted or referred to by witnesses or writers of oral history. In some cases, though, to move the story along, I have inserted a word or a sentence or two, which, though not recorded, do seem to me to be true to the story.

Kamehameha's remark to Kotzebue regarding his religion is found in Kotzebue's book.

Kamehameha's and Vancouver's discussion about which is the true religion was described by Ebenezer Townsend, Jr., of the *Neptune* in 1798, as told to him by John Young, who had acted as interpreter between Kamehameha and Vancouver. See Judd.

NOTES

The gravity demonstration was described by a Russian naval officer, Captain Golovnin. A translation was published in *The Friend* in July and August 1894.

Hawai'i and Great Britain

Though Vancouver wholeheartedly believed that he had convinced Kamehameha to give the island of Hawai'i to Great Britain, it is doubtful that this was Kamehameha's understanding. Rather, it is thought that he assumed his treaty with Vancouver meant that his kingdom would be protected by Great Britain in the event of foreign conflict. See Golovnin and Westervelt.

MELE INOA

Hanau ke alii Kekuiapoiwa.
I nakolo ka lani.
I Welehu ka malama
I kulia i lalapa maloko Ainakea.
Kokohi ke maloko ilaila
Hanau kalani nui mehameha
Ka hooeli o ke kapu.
Ke pulikoliko o ke kapu.
I naha maloko mai o Ainakea
I eweewe alii i lalapa
Maloko o Kekuiapoiwa
O ka Mano nui kapu lalakea
O ke alii o ka pali nui kiekie
O Malu ka lani, he kaha na Awini
E hii ana ia kalani nui mehameha
Me he hulu nene la ka haki manawa
O ka pali e ku nei
He uli huna Malu no Paiea
Kaha hulaana na Awini
I hoao ana me Keahialaka
Ke o o Paiea alii e o e.

Kekuiapoiwa, the chiefess, gave birth
The heavens rumbled
Welehu was the month
(Life) was kindled and blazed inside of Ainakea
The light was shaded there
The great chief Kamehameha was born
With the deepest kapu
The highest kapu
Breaking forth at Ainakea

71

Of a family of chiefs that blazed forth
From within Kekuiapoiwa
A great, sacred, white-finned shark
A chief of the great, tall cliff
Sheltered was the heavenly one at the land of Awini
There the great chief Kamehameha was borne in the arms
Like the feather of a goose
To the sheer cliff that stands there yet
A dark shady spot to hide Paiea
On the inaccessible cliff of Awini
That is wedded to Keahialaka
Answer to thy name chant, O chief Paiea.

This chant is about the birth of Kamehameha, classified by the Bishop Museum as a *mele inoa*. The Hawaiian version appeared in the *Ka Nupepa Kuokoa*, June 9, 1911, page 7. The translation is by Mary Kawena Pukui (1895–1986) and can be found in the Bishop Museum Archives, MS SC Pukui, Box 17.4. Pukui chose to delete punctuation from her translation, and neither version was written with diacritical marks. Diacritical marks in the chant fragment in Chapter 2 were inserted by the author.

IMPORTANT DATES IN KAMEHAMEHA'S LIFE

1758 Kamehameha was born in the district of Kohala on the island of Hawai'i. (Most sources place it somewhere between 1736 and 1761, but Halley's Comet's appearance in 1758 provides an explanation for the bright star that shone over his birth; therefore, this date is accepted by many.)

1775 Overturning the Naha Stone may have occurred around this year, as well as the battle on Maui where Kamehameha saved his warrior-teacher, Kekūhaupi'o.

1778 Captain James Cook first visited the islands (January 18).

1779 Captain James Cook was killed at Kealakekua Bay (February 14).

1785 Kamehameha married Ka'ahumanu.

1792 Kamehameha became king of the island of Hawai'i.

1794 Kahekili died in Waikīkī (June).

1795 Maui, Moloka'i, Kaho'olawe, and Lāna'i fell to Kamehameha, followed by O'ahu.

1797 Kamehameha's sacred wife, Keōpūolani, gave birth to Liholiho in Hilo.

1810 Kaumuali'i ceded Kaua'i to Kamehameha. Kamehameha had now united the Hawaiian Islands.

1819 King Kamehameha the Great died in Kona (May 8).

GLOSSARY

ALAPAʻI High chief on the island of Hawaiʻi at the time of
Kamehameha's birth.

ALBATROSS American trading ship commanded by Nathan Winship.

ALIʻI Royalty; of the nobility.

ʻAWEOWEO Hawaiian species of red fish.

ʻĀWINI Land in Kohala, where Kamehameha was taken after his birth.

BRITANNIA Ship built for Kamehameha by order of George
Vancouver.

CANTON Chinese port open to foreigners, a destination of the trading
ships.

CHATHAM A ship under George Vancouver's command during his
visits to the Hawaiian Islands.

CHORIS, LOUIS Ship's artist on the Russian ship *Rurick* under the
command of Lieutenant Otto von Kotzebue. He painted a well-
known portrait of Kamehameha in 1816, three years before Kamehameha's death.

COOK, JAMES British naval captain who, in January 1778, was the first
known Westerner to visit Hawaiʻi. Kamehameha visited aboard his
ship and also witnessed his death.

DAVIS, ISAAC Englishman aboard the American trading ship *Fair
American,* who became one of Kamehameha's close advisors.

DISCOVERY One of Captain Cook's ships in Hawaiʻi, commanded at
the time by Captain Charles Clerke.

DISCOVERY Sloop commanded by George Vancouver. (Not the same
ship as Cook's.)

ELEANORA American trading vessel commanded by Simon Metcalfe,
of which John Young had been a crew member. Kamehameha's first
cannon came from this ship.

FAIR AMERICAN Sailing ship that was commanded by Thomas Metcalfe and of which Isaac Davis had been a crew member.

GLOSSARY

GEORGE III King of Great Britain from 1760 to 1820.

HALEMAʻUMAʻU Volcano crater within the larger crater of Kīlauea on the island of Hawaiʻi.

HĀNA Village in east Maui. Birthplace of Kaʻahumanu.

HAWAIʻI Largest of the Hawaiian islands. Also known as the Big Island. Birthplace and home of Kamehameha.

HEIAU Temple of worship.

HONOLULU Village on Oʻahu with a navigable harbor, which became an important trading center during Kamehameha's reign.

ʻĪAO Narrow, high-peaked valley in Maui, where a decisive battle was fought between Kamehameha and Kalanikūpule and was named the Damming of the Waters, or *Kepaniwai*.

ʻIʻIWI Scarlet forest bird whose feathers were used for cloaks and other featherwork. Hawaiian honeycreeper.

ʻIKUWĀ Month near the end of the year, named for the roar of the surf, thunder, and cloudbursts that take place during this time.

KAʻAHUMANU Kamehameha's favorite wife, born in Hāna.

KĀʻEO Half-brother of Kahekili and once the high chief of Kauaʻi.

KAHEKILI Fierce warrior and high chief of Maui, who many believe to have been the father of Kamehameha.

KĀHILI Feather staff, symbol of royalty.

KAHU Guardian, honored attendant.

KAHUNA Hawaiian priest. Expert in a subject, such as religion, astronomy, or medicine.

KAIANA Chief who betrayed Kamehameha.

KAILUA-KONA Area on the leeward side of Hawaiʻi, where Kamehameha spent his last years.

KALANIKŪPULE Son of Kahekili and high chief of Oʻahu. May have been Kamehameha's half-brother.

KALANIʻŌPUʻU Kamehameha's uncle, who became king of Hawaiʻi after Alapaʻi.

KANALOA Hawaiian god of the sea.

KĀNE Hawaiian god of life, sunlight, and fresh water.

GLOSSARY

KAPA Cloth made from pounding the bark of the mulberry tree and other trees, such as breadfruit.

KAPU Taboo; to be forbidden.

KA'Ū District on the southeastern side of Hawai'i.

KAUA'I Northernmost of the major Hawaiian islands, and the last island to come under Kamehameha's control in 1810.

KAUIKEAOULI Kamehameha's second royal son (1814–1854). Became Kamehameha III in 1824.

KAUMUALI'I King of Kaua'i, who ceded the island to Kamehameha in 1810.

KAWAIOLALOA One of Kamehameha's horses.

KEALAKEKUA BAY Bay on the island of Hawai'i, where Captain Cook was killed in 1779.

KE'EAUMOKU Chief and one of Kamehameha's most trusted counselors. Father of Ka'ahumanu.

KEKŪHAUPI'O Chief who trained Kamehameha in the arts of war.

KEKU'IAPOIWA Kamehameha's mother.

KEŌPŪOLANI Kamehameha's highest-born wife, who was the mother of Liholiho, Kauikeaouli, and Nāhi'ena'ena. She was the niece of Kahekili.

KEŌUA A chief of Hawai'i, husband of Keku'iapoiwa, and brother of Kalani'ōpu'u. Kamehameha's acknowledged father, although many believe his father was Kahekili.

KEŌUA Second son of Kalani'ōpu'u.

KEPANIWAI The battle of 'Īao Valley, the Damming of the Waters.

KEPŪWAHA'ULA'ULA The Battle of the Red-Mouthed Gun.

KĪ Ti plant. Leafy Polynesian plant whose leaves were used for thatch roofs, rain capes, skirts, sandals, and other garments.

KĪLAUEA Volcano on the island of Hawai'i.

KIWALA'Ō Eldest son of Kalani'ōpu'u.

KOA Tree that grows in the forests of Hawai'i and whose wood is prized for canoes, paddles, bowls, and furniture.

KOHALA District in northern Hawai'i, birthplace of Kamehameha.

KONA The leeward, or western, side of the island of Hawai'i.

KŪ Shortened name of the war god, Kūkā'ilimoku.

KŪKĀ'ILIMOKU Kū, fierce Hawaiian god of war.

LĀNA'I Island between Maui and Moloka'i.

LAW OF THE SPLINTERED PADDLE Law proclaimed by Kamehameha to protect the rights of his people.

LIHOLIHO Kamehameha's eldest royal son, who became Kamehameha II on Kamehameha's death in 1819.

LONO God of agriculture and of the harvest.

MALO Loincloth.

MAMO Mostly black forest bird, whose yellow feathers above and below the tail were used in featherwork. Honeycreeper.

MANA Supernatural or divine power.

MARIN, FRANCISCO DE PAULA Spaniard who came to Hawai'i in the early 1790s and was a close friend and advisor of Kamehameha for many years.

MAUI Hawaiian island closest to Hawai'i, ruled over by Kahekili.

MOLOKA'I Island between Maui and O'ahu.

NAE'OLE Kohala chief who carried the infant Kamehameha to 'Āwini and was his guardian for five years.

NAHA STONE Large sacred stone of which it was said that the man who could move it would become king.

NĀHI'ENA'ENA Kamehameha's third royal child, a daughter (1815–1836).

NI'IHAU Island near Kaua'i. One of the eight major Hawaiian islands.

NORTHWEST PASSAGE A sea route above the northern coast of North America connecting the Atlantic Ocean to the Pacific Ocean. Many expeditions searched for this route, hoping to shorten the trade routes to China and India.

NU'UANU Valley on O'ahu where Kamehameha defeated Kalanikūpule and gained control of O'ahu. Site of the Battle of Nu'uanu.

NU'UANU PALI Cliff at the head of Nu'uanu Valley, where Kamehameha's warriors forced many of the enemy to fall to their death.

O'AHU One of the eight major Hawaiian islands, conquered by Kamehameha in 1895.

OLONĀ Hawaiian shrub whose bark is twisted into a strong fiber for making nets.

'Ō'Ō Black forest bird with yellow feathers prized for cloaks, helmets, and other featherwork. Now extinct, except perhaps on Kaua'i.

PAI'EA A small, edible crab. Name given to Kamehameha for the first years of his life.

PELE Goddess of the volcano. Said to reside in Halema'uma'u Crater.

POI Smooth, starchy paste made from the taro root. An important food source for Hawaiians.

PU'UKOHOLĀ *Heiau* near Kawaihae, Kohala, built by Kamehameha for his war god, Kūkā'ilimoku.

RESOLUTION Cook's flagship at the time of his discovery of the Hawaiian Islands, January 18, 1778.

SHALER, WILLIAM American trader who brought the first horses to the islands in 1803 from California. In 1805, he sold Kamehameha the *Lelia Byrd*, which became Kamehameha's flagship.

UNION JACK The flag of Great Britain.

VANCOUVER, GEORGE British naval captain and explorer who visited the Hawaiian islands several times between 1792 and 1794 and was a friend of Kamehameha.

WAI'ALAE One of Kamehameha's landing places for the invasion of O'ahu.

WAIKĪKĪ Village on O'ahu's south shore. One of Kamehameha's landing places for the invasion of O'ahu, and later the site of one of his residences.

WAIPI'O Valley in northern Hawai'i where Kalani'ōpu'u held a ceremony naming his son Kiwala'ō as his heir and Kamehameha as the keeper of the war god.

WAUKE Paper mulberry, a small tree whose bark was used for *kapa*.

WINSHIP, NATHAN American sea captain who was responsible for bringing Kaumuali'i to meet with Kamehameha and who bore him

back to Kaua'i, helping him to avoid treachery at the hands of
Kamehameha's men.

YOUNG, JOHN Englishman aboard the American trading ship
Eleanora who become one of Kamehameha's close advisors and
the governor of the island of Hawai'i. His granddaughter, Emma,
became the wife of Kamehameha IV.

Definitions of Hawaiian words taken from *New Pocket Hawaiian Dictionary,* by Mary Kawena Pukui and Samuel H. Elbert, with Esther T. Mookini and Yu Mapuana Nishizawa
(Honolulu: University of Hawai'i Press, 1992).

BIBLIOGRAPHY

Alexander, William De Witt. "The Birth of Kamehameha I." *Nineteenth Annual Report of the Hawaiian Historical Society for 1911,* 6–8.

Barrère, Dorothy B. *Kamehameha in Kona: Two Documentary Studies.* Pacific Anthropological Records No. 23. Honolulu: Bernice P. Bishop Museum, 1975.

Bingham, Hiram. *A Residence of Twenty-One Years in the Sandwich Islands.* Hartford: Hezekiah Huntington, 1847.

Bradley, Harold. *American Frontier in Hawaii: The Pioneers, 1789–1843.* Gloucester, Mass.: Peter Smith, 1968.

Campbell, Archibald. *Voyage Round the World, 1806–1812.* Honolulu: University of Hawai'i Press, 1967.

Conrad, Agnes C. *The Letters and Journals of Francisco.* Honolulu: University of Hawai'i Press, 1973.

Cook, James. *The Voyages of the* Resolution *and* Discovery, *1776–1780.* Vol. III of *The Journals of Captain Cook.* Ed. J. C. Beaglehole. Cambridge: Published for the Hakluyt Society at the University Press, 1967.

Corney, Peter. *Early Voyages in the North Pacific, 1813–1818.* Fairfield, Wash.: Ye Galleon Press, 1965.

Daws, Gavan. *Shoal of Time: A History of the Hawaiian Islands.* Toronto: The MacMillan Co., 1968.

de Vis-Norton, Lionel W. *The Story of the Naha Stone.* Adapted from the translation of an old document. Hilo: Board of Trade, n.d.

Dibble, Sheldon. *A History of the Sandwich Islands.* Honolulu: Thomas G. Thrumm, 1909.

Ellis, William. *Journal of William Ellis: Narrative of a Tour of Hawaii.* Honolulu: Advertiser Publishing Co., 1963.

Feher, Joseph, Edward Joesting, and O. A. Bushnell. *Hawaii: A Pictorial History.* Honolulu: Bishop Museum Press, 1969.

Gast, Ross H., and Agnes Conrad. "The Letters and Journals of Francisco," in *Don Francisco de Paula Marin, A Biography.* Honolulu: University of Hawai'i Press, 1973.

BIBLIOGRAPHY

Golovnin, V. M. *Around the World on the* Kamschatka, *1817–1819.* Translated by Ella Lury Wiswell. Honolulu: The Hawaiian Historical Society and the University Press of Hawai'i, 1979.

I'i, John Papa. *Fragments of Hawaiian History.* Translated by Mary K. Pukui and edited by Dorothy B. Barrère. Honolulu: Bishop Museum Press, 1959.

Jarves, James J. *History of the Hawaiian Islands.* Honolulu: Henry M. Whitney, Publisher, 1872.

Joesting, Edward. *Hawaii: An Uncommon History.* New York: W. W. Norton & Co., 1972.

Judd, Walter F. *Kamehameha.* Norfolk Island, Australia: Hawaiian Bicentennial Library, Island Heritage Limited, 1976.

Kalakaua, David. *The Myths and Legends of Hawaii.* Rutland, Vt.: Charles E. Tuttle Co., 1972.

Kamakau, Samuel M. *Ruling Chiefs of Hawaii.* Honolulu: Kamehameha Schools Press, 1961.

Kotzebue, Otto von. *A Voyage of Discovery into the South Sea and the Beering's Straits, Vol. 1.* New York: Da Capo Press, 1967.

Kuykendall, Ralph S. *The Hawaiian Kingdom, Vol. 1, 1778–1854.* Honolulu: University of Hawai'i Press, 1938.

Makemson, Dr. Maud W. "The Legend of Koko-iki and the Birthday of Kamehameha I." *Forty-fourth Annual Report of the Hawaiian Historical Society for 1935.*

Malo, David. *Hawaiian Antiquities.* Translated by Nathaniel B. Emerson. Honolulu: Star Bulletin Press, 1951.

Pukui, Mary Kawena, Samuel H. Elbert, and Esther T. Mookini. *New Pocket Hawaiian Dictionary.* Honolulu: University of Hawai'i Press, 1992.

Pukui, Mary Kawena, Samuel H. Elbert, and Esther T. Mookini. *Place Names of Hawaii.* Honolulu: University of Hawai'i Press, 1974.

"Report to the Hawaiian Historical Society by Its Trustees Concerning the Birth Date of Kamehameha I and Kamehameha Day Celebrations." *Forty-fourth Annual Report of the Hawaiian Historical Society for 1935.*

BIBLIOGRAPHY

Starbuck, Peter. "The Legends of Kamehameha." Master's thesis in English, University of Hawai'i, 1979.

Stewart, C. S. *Journal of a Residence in the Sandwich Islands, 1823, 1824, and 1825.* Honolulu: University of Hawai'i Press, 1970.

Stokes, John F. G. "New Bases for Hawaiian Chronology." *Forty-first Annual Report of the Hawaiian Historical Society for 1932.*

Tatar, Elizabeth. *nineteenth century hawaiian chant.* Pacific Anthropological Records No. 33. Honolulu: Department of Anthropology, Bernice P. Bishop Museum, March 1982.

Vancouver, George. *Voyage of Discovery to the North Pacific Ocean and Round the World, Vol. 3.* New York: Da Capo Press, 1967.

Westervelt, W. D. "Kamehameha's Cession of the Island of Hawaii to Great Britain in 1794." *Twenty-second Annual Report of the Hawaiian Historical Society for 1913.*

ABOUT THE AUTHOR

Susan Morrison, a Hawai'i resident and educator, has a special interest in Hawaiian history and culture. She is a contributor to *Notable Women of Hawai'i* and *Hawai'i Chronicles,* and her writing has appeared in both Hawai'i and national magazines.

ABOUT THE ILLUSTRATOR

Karen Kiefer was raised in Hawai'i and currently lives in Kailua as an artist and art educator.